This book belongs to

_____

_____

This edition published by Parragon Books Ltd in 2014

Parragon Books Ltd
Chartist House
15–17 Trim Street
Bath BA1 1HA, UK
www.parragon.com

ISBN 978-1-4723-8187-3

Printed in China

Disney MOVIE COLLECTION
A SPECIAL DISNEY STORYBOOK SERIES

THE LION KING

Bath • New York • Cologne • Melbourne • Delhi
Hong Kong • Shenzhen • Singapore • Amsterdam

The hot African sun rose on an amazing sight. Giraffes, zebras, elephants and animals of all kinds were gathered at Pride Rock. This was an important day. King Mufasa and Queen Sarabi had invited the wise old baboon, Rafiki, to present their newborn cub to the animal kingdom. Rafiki ceremoniously marked the cub's forehead with coloured dust. Then he lifted the infant high into the air for all to see. The animals cheered and bowed before Prince Simba.

But one family member didn't attend the celebration – Mufasa's brother, Scar.

Mufasa and his assistant, Zazu, went to ask Scar why he had missed the presentation.

Zazu reminded Scar that, as the king's brother, he should have been first in line to congratulate the family.

"I was the first in line until the little hairball was born," retorted Scar, angry that he was no longer heir to the throne.

"That 'hairball' is my son, and your future king," Mufasa growled as Scar walked away.

As time went by, Simba grew into a playful and curious cub.
Early one morning, Mufasa brought Simba to the top of
Pride Rock. "Everything the light touches is our kingdom,"
he told his son. "One day the sun will set on my time here
and will rise with you as the new king."

"Wow!" cried Simba. "But what about that shadowy place?"

"That is beyond our borders. You must never go there,"
said Mufasa, sternly.

"But I thought a king could do whatever he wants," said Simba.

"There's more to being king than getting your way all the time," Mufasa explained. "You need to respect all creatures. We are all connected in the great circle of life."

Simba tried to listen but he was busy chasing grasshoppers and practising his pounce.

Just then, Zazu appeared, urgently warning the king
that dangerous hyenas had crossed into the Pride Lands!
Simba begged his father to let him go with him,
but Mufasa simply commanded Zazu to take Simba
home as he sped off to protect the kingdom.
"I never get to go anywhere," Simba complained.

Back at home, Simba went to see his uncle Scar.

"My dad just showed me the whole kingdom," the cub bragged. "And I'm gonna rule it all!"

Scar scowled. Then, slowly, he began to smile.

"Did he show you that place beyond the border?" asked Scar slyly. "Only the bravest of lions would dare to go to an elephant graveyard."

Simba didn't see his uncle's evil trap. He decided to show his father what a brave cub he could be.

Simba found his best friend, Nala, with her mother and Queen Sarabi.

"I just heard about this great place! Can Nala and I go?" Simba asked Sarabi. "It's near the watering hole," he fibbed.

"All right," said Sarabi, "as long as Zazu goes with you."

Not Zazu! thought Simba. He'll spoil everything!

As they set off, Simba whispered to Nala. "We've got to ditch Zazu! We're really going to an elephant graveyard!"

He and Nala darted through herds of animals until they left Zazu far behind.

"We lost Zazu!" Simba exclaimed. "Now we can look for the elephant graveyard!"

As he and Nala wandered, they tumbled downhill and landed with a thud … next to a huge elephant skull. They were in the graveyard.

"It's really creepy," Nala said.

"Let's check it out," Simba said.

But soon Zazu caught up with the adventurous cubs. "We're way beyond the boundary of the Pride Lands," he scolded. "And we are in very real danger!"

At that moment, three hyenas named Banzai, Shenzi and Ed slunk towards them from inside the skull.

Terrified, the cubs ran for their lives. As they darted and stumbled across piles of old elephant bones, Nala suddenly slipped and fell.

Shenzi lunged at her, but Simba swiped his sharp claws across the hyena's cheek.

Suddenly, a tremendous roar shook the ground.
It was Mufasa!
His giant paw struck one of the hyenas as he
growled, "If you ever come near my son again…."
The hyenas ran away before he could finish.
No one noticed Scar lurking in the shadows.

Mufasa scolded his son on the way home. "You disobeyed me, Simba."
"I was just trying to be brave, like you, Dad," said Simba softly.
"Being brave doesn't mean you go looking for trouble," replied Mufasa.
While they talked, Mufasa directed Simba's attention up to the stars.
"The great kings of the past look down on us from those stars," Mufasa
explained. "Just remember that those kings will always be there to guide
you … and so will I."

Later that night, Scar visited the hyenas.
"I practically gift-wrapped those cubs for you and you couldn't even dispose of them," he said with a sneer.

"What were we supposed to do? Kill Mufasa?" Banzai whined.

"Precisely," answered Scar. Then he told them of his new plan. This time, no one would escape.

The next day, Scar found Simba.

"Your father has a surprise for you," he said. Scar led
Simba down a steep gorge and told him to wait there.

Then Scar signalled the hyenas to frighten a herd of wildebeests.
The panicked animals stampeded right towards Simba.
Hearing the thundering hooves, Mufasa looked into the gorge
and saw his son. He leaped down and saved Simba's life.

Simba was safe but Mufasa was still in danger. As he tried to climb away from the stampede, the rocks crumbled beneath him.

Struggling up the cliff, Mufasa saw Scar. "Brother, help me!" Mufasa cried.

Scar dug his sharp claws into Mufasa's paws and whispered, "Long live the king!" Then he let go. Mufasa fell and disappeared beneath the herd below.

Simba hadn't seen Scar push Mufasa, he had only seen his father fall.

When the stampede was gone, Simba ran to Mufasa.

"Dad? Dad?" Simba cried, nuzzling him. But his father lay motionless. The great king was dead.

Scar came to Simba's side. "If it weren't for you," he said, "your father would still be alive! Run away and never return!"

Heartbroken, poor Simba ran away as fast as he could.

Scar sent the hyenas out to kill Simba, but the cub escaped them once more.

The hyenas lied to Scar, telling him Simba was dead.

At Pride Rock, Scar told the grieving lionesses the news.

"It is with a heavy heart," he lied, "that I become your new king!"

Rafiki and Sarabi listened in disbelief.

Everyone in the Pride Lands mourned for their beloved king and Simba.

Meanwhile, Simba was far away from the Pride Lands. The ground turned dry and cracked beneath him. The hot sun beat down as vultures circled above his head.

Exhausted and unable to go any further, Simba slumped to the ground.

After a long while, Simba awoke. Everything around him looked different. Instead of desert, there were trees, grass and flowers.

A meerkat named Timon and a warthog named Pumbaa had brought him to their home.

"You nearly died," said Pumbaa.

"We saved you!" cried Timon.

Simba stood up, thanked Timon and Pumbaa and started to leave.

Pumbaa asked Simba where he was from, but Simba didn't want to answer. "I did something terrible ... but I don't want to talk about it."

"You gotta put your troubles behind you, kid," said Timon. "No past, no future, no worries ... hakuna matata!"

Timon and Pumbaa's happy-go-lucky attitude quickly cheered Simba.
He decided to stay with his new friends.

Years passed and Simba grew into a young lion.

One night, while looking up at the stars with his friends, Simba remembered his father's words. "Someone once told me that the great kings of the past are up there, watching over us," he said to his friends.

Suddenly wanting to be alone, Simba wandered off. As he sat gazing at the sky, his paw broke a bit of milkweed fluff. Caught in the night breeze, it drifted away …

… until it reached Rafiki's tree. The old baboon plucked the fluff from the air and sniffed it.

"Simba!" the old baboon exclaimed. "It is time!"

Rafiki painted a red mane around a lion cub etched on a tree. Then he walked into the darkness in search of Simba.

The next day, Pumbaa was chasing a bug when a fierce lioness sprang at him from the tall grass. He screamed and tried to run away, but he got stuck beneath a fallen tree.

"She's gonna eat me!" he squealed. As Timon tried to push Pumbaa free, Simba rushed to help.

Simba wrestled with the lioness, but then he realized she was his old friend, Nala.

"You're alive!" Nala said happily. "That means you're the king!"

Nala told Simba how Scar had destroyed the Pride Lands. "Scar let the hyenas take over. There's no food, no water. Simba, you're our only hope."

"I can't go back," said Simba angrily. He turned and walked away.

Simba thought about what Nala had said. "I won't go back," he said to himself. "It won't change anything."

Just then, Simba heard a chanting song from the jungle. Rafiki came walking towards him. "If you want to see your father again, look down there," Rafiki said, pointing into the pool of water next to them. Simba stared and saw Mufasa's face reflected in the pool.

"He lives in you!" Rafiki said.

Suddenly, Mufasa's image appeared in the clouds.
His voice seemed to fill Simba's mind and heart.
    "You must take your place in the circle of life.
Remember who you are. You are my son and the
one true king."
    As the vision faded, Simba knew what he must do.

The next morning, Rafiki told Timon, Pumbaa and Nala that Simba had returned to the Pride Lands.

"He's gone back to challenge Scar!" Nala exclaimed joyfully.

When Simba reached the Pride Lands, he was saddened by what he saw. His homeland, once green and beautiful, had turned barren under Scar's rule.

Bravely, Simba continued on his journey.

When Simba arrived at Pride Rock, he let out a roar
that shook the earth. Scar was surprised and frightened.
He thought the hyenas had killed Simba long ago.

"This is my kingdom!" shouted Simba. "Step down, Scar."

Scar lunged. Simba stepped back, lost his footing and
slipped off the cliff.

As Simba clung to the cliff edge, Scar leaned over him.
"Now this looks familiar," he said with a sneer. "Oh yes!
I remember. This is just the way your father looked before he died."
Scar smiled evilly.

Then Simba realized that it had been Scar who killed his father!

Outraged, Simba gathered his strength, sprang back on to the rock and attacked.
At that moment, Nala, Timon and Pumbaa arrived and a battle broke out
on Pride Rock.

Suddenly – CRACK! – lightning struck the dry grasslands. In seconds, huge
flames roared around Pride Rock.

Scar tried to sneak away, but Simba cornered him at the top of Pride Rock.
"Run away, Scar," Simba said, repeating what Scar had told him long ago.
"Run away and never return!"

But Scar lunged at Simba. With a powerful swipe of his great paw,
Simba knocked Scar off the cliff and he fell to his death in the gorge below.

As rain began to fall, drenching the flames, Simba stood at the top of
Pride Rock and roared triumphantly.

Simba took his rightful place as the Lion King and in time the Pride Lands flourished once again. Grass and trees grew, herds returned to graze and food was plentiful.

Soon all the animals gathered at Pride Rock to celebrate the birth of Simba and Nala's cub. The circle of life would continue.

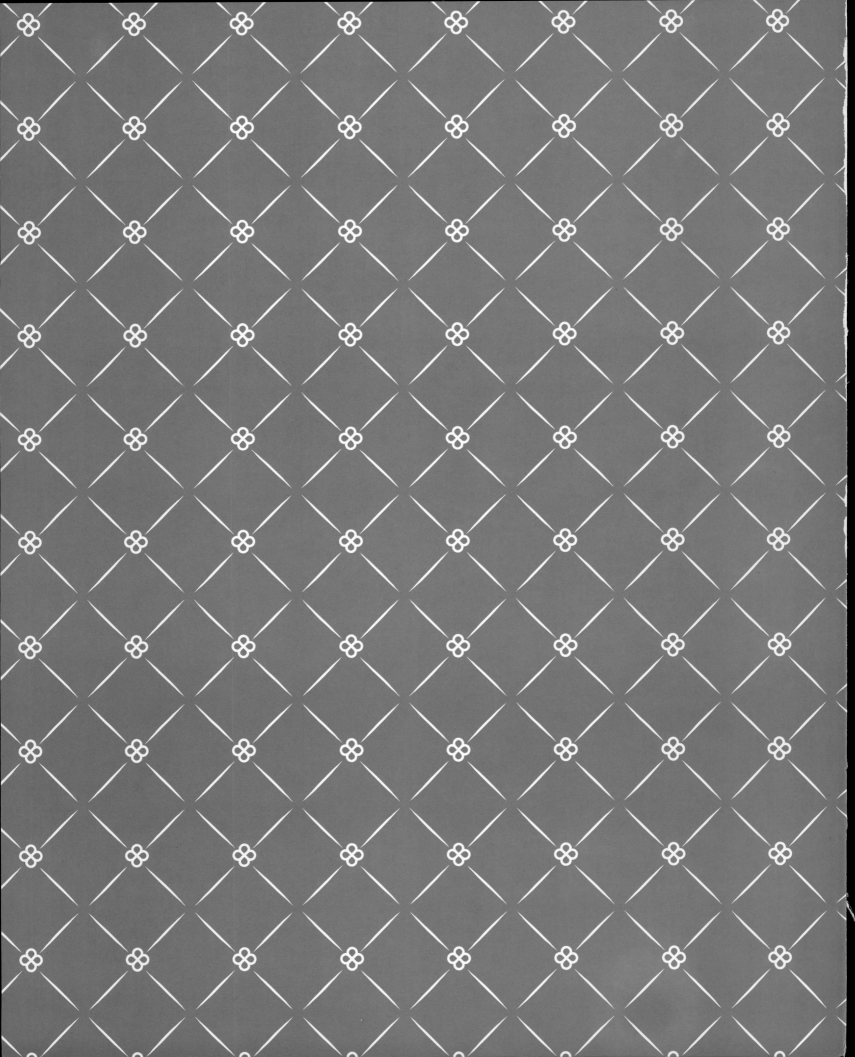